# SINJAB AND SASHA

## LOVE IN CHIRRING WOODS

MONA ADHAMI

*For my mother. For supporting my journey of learning, reading, and writing.*

# TABLE OF CONTENTS

# CHAPTER 1: PLAYFUL POUNCE

I lay crouched amidst the green blades of grass, my body snug to the earth. Peering out with wide eyes, I spotted her hopping joyfully along, her long fluffy tail moving like a wave behind her. I could hear her humming. I smelled her scent of acorns and berries.

"Patience," I whispered to myself. "Wait for it."

She slowly approached until she was within a leap's distance.

"Now!"

I sprang out from my hiding place and playfully pounced upon her. She gasped with surprise as we tumbled and rolled together on the grass. When she realized it was me, she giggled uncontrollably.

"Oh, Sinjab! How many times are you going to sneak up on me like that?" she asked. I laughed and responded, "How many times am I going to catch you off guard, Sasha? You gotta keep you're guard up."

She tousled my brownish-gray fur with her slender paws and smiled. Her big black eyes became lost in mine as we lay entangled in one another's arms. I could feel her warmth and hear her breathing. Her long whiskers brushed up against mine.

"But you'll always be there for me, won't you Sinjab? To protect me?"

The way she looked at me was worth a million acorns. A look of admiration mixed with love and romantic longing.

I grinned and replied, "Always." I rubbed my nose against hers and kissed her soft, delicate lips.

With her arms around my neck, she said, "I don't know what I'd do without you. Don't ever leave me, Sinjab."

I shook my head and replied, "I won't."

After a moment of silence, she said, "I bet I can beat you to the pond."

"Only if I give you a head start."

"What is that supposed to mean?"

I released her from my loving grasp and walked circles around her. "If I go easy on you, you might just stand a chance."

She growled and made a clawing motion with her paw. "You're just afraid you'll lose."

"Nah, I don't lose to girls."

"Then let's race. On your mark, get set...," Sasha said as she bounded off towards the pond.

"Cheater!" I yelled from behind.

I darted forward, hopping through the grass as I slowly gained momentum. I leaped through the field like an acrobat jumping from a trampoline. Every time my paws hit the earth, I felt I bolt of energy rush through me, propelling me forward.

I passed by Sasha, glanced over, and said, "Meet you at the pond."

I had to win the race. Losing was not an option. I had to prove to Sasha that I was in charge. Always was and always would be. I gave it one final push and sped along until I reached the edge of the pond. I stood there with my arms crossed, head tilted to one side. After a long while, Sasha arrived, out of breath and flustered.

"What took you so long?" I asked. "I've been waiting here for ages now."

Breathing heavily, she replied, "It's because I was going easy on you." She wiped the sweat from her forehead.

"You know the pond is over here, not down there," I joked. "But you put up a good fight."

"I'll win next time. Just you wait."

And just as I embraced her with my arms, the woods embraced us with its calming colors. A placid pond reflected towering trees in the height of their autumn foliage. Splashes of yellow and red could be seen dispersed among the trees which formed a kind of protective canopy overhead. Small crimson bushes resembling flames flanked the pond while strokes of amber leaves lay brushed across the green meadow. The woods were like a paint palette of autumn colors.

We felt a gentle breeze dance through the woods. It approached ever so slowly, almost as if it sought permission to enter upon our sanctuary. We heard the rustling of leaves and the chirping of birds.

"Sinjab, won't you take me up to the treetops again?" Sasha requested. "I want to see the sunset again."

"I think the one standing next to me is brighter than the sun. But sure."

I took her by the paw and led her up the trees. We jumped from branch to branch, the soft leaves brushing up against our fur. Reaching the very top, we felt a kind of serenity descend upon us as we watched the sun's orange rays suffuse the horizon. A panoramic view of the woods presented itself to us. She curled up against me, her head nestled against my shoulder. As we sat snuggled together on the highest branch, I wrapped my tail around hers.

"I'm happy here in the woods with you," she whispered in my ear.

"I'm happy with you too, Sasha," I responded.

"I remember, I was scared to come here from the other side of town. But with all the trees cut down, I couldn't stay there anymore."

"I'm glad you made the journey. Life was dull before you came along."

"Do you remember the first time we met?"

"How could I ever forget? You were like a ballerina leaping through the meadows," I reminisced as I tightened my tail's grasp around hers.

"I must have caught your eye real good. In just two weeks, you proposed to me. You kept chasing me around the whole woods until I accepted! And almost one year later, here we are."

I thought back to those days when Sasha and I first met. She was such a beauty. She brought a kind of positive energy wherever she went. I was initially hesitant to propose to her, knowing very well that other male squirrels stood a better chance than I did. Competition that was stronger, taller, and more established than I was. Proposing to Sasha was probably the bravest thing I had ever done in my life. Even though I feared rejection, I told myself that I had nothing to lose and everything to gain. I wanted to be with her. And when she accepted my proposal, I was honestly surprised. I thought I was just going to make a fool of myself, but apparently she loved me back.

"Sinjab, tell me that you love me," she gently requested as she nuzzled my neck.

I looked her in the eyes, and said, "I love you, Sasha."

"I love you too, Sinjab."

I kissed her and brought her even closer under my arm. And as the sun slowly sank away, the day came to an end.

# CHAPTER 2:

# MORNING IN THE MEADOWS

We awoke in the hollow of our large oak tree which overlooked the rest of the woods. It was an old, gnarled tree reaching high up into the sky. A majestic oak which had stood for centuries amongst the other trees, and for the past year, it had protected me and Sinjab from the cold and rain. Not only did the oak tree provide us with shelter, but also comfort, security, and a home to call our own.

Its strong branches, laden with brilliant red leaves, twisted left and right. Its bark was soft against our claws, its leaves comforting to our eyes, and its redolent scent of acorns soothing to our senses.

Our den was wide and spacious for both of us, conveniently situated at the top of the tree. I had taken it upon myself to furnish the hollow when Sinjab and I first moved in. A small rug lay in the center with a rocking chair on one end and our bed on the other.

Above our bookshelf, a sign on the wall read *Chirring Woods* which had acorns on the frame. I had also hung up some violet roses from the ceiling as décor.

Another day of foraging awaited us. With winter fast approaching, we needed to find more acorns to bury. We scampered down our tree to find a trove of acorns sprinkled across the meadows. It was like an all-you-can-eat buffet staring right at us. We descended upon the acorns with rapacious appetites.

As I stood gnawing at an acorn, Sinjab asked, "Have your front teeth grown longer?"

I felt my cheeks burn. "I didn't think you would notice," I responded shyly.

"How *couldn't* I notice?" he said, winking at me.

I smiled coquettishly and looked down. After a few moments, I looked back up to see him grinning, his eyes glued on me. We became lost in one another's gaze. His charm captivated me as I felt my heart beat faster and my cheeks burn hotter.

He stood up tall to survey the meadow, his bushy tail arched behind him. The white fur on his underside glistened in the sun. His sharp nose and whiskers twitched slightly as he analyzed all the various scents in the meadow.

It was always fun with Sinjab around. There was never a dull moment in my life after I married him. I felt happy when he was around, and even the simplest things he said or did made me giggle and smile. I felt safe and protected with Sinjab by my side. Just hearing his voice was enough to abate the sadness I felt on gloomy days.

As I absorbed the romantic moment, a voice called out from the trees. "Enjoying breakfast down there, I see?"

We looked up to see Mrs. Tayra. She hopped about on the branches, chirping and fluttering her wings. I nodded my head in acknowledgement.

Sinjab looked up. "Well, if it isn't Mrs. Tayra. How have you been?"

"Been busy with the little ones. Young Jack is about ready to fly any day now."

"I don't doubt he'll be an amazing flyer just like his mother."

"Oh, why thank you, Sinjab. That means a lot."

My eyes widened as I watched the scene unravel before me. I felt my breathing stop momentarily as my lips pursed together. A smoldering jealousy seized me as I felt hot blood pulse through my body and my tail twitch.

*My* husband conversing with another woman. The sight disgusted me. I wanted this silly bird gone forever. I considered throwing an acorn at her to shoo her away, but I thought Sinjab would deem it uncivilized or even unladylike. I would not have his opinion of me tarnished by some dumb bird.

"He almost fell out of the nest the other day. It was a good thing I was close by to catch him," continued Mrs. Tayra. "But how is everything, Sinjab?"

The audacity she had to intrude upon our foraging with her stupid orange feathers. And that beak! It was about to knock someone in the face! It was almost a hazard. Every time I heard her say the name Sinjab, it was like a sword piercing my heart.

"We're preparing for the winter. Always good to store a little bit extra," Sinjab said.

Mrs. Tayra must have sensed I was in no mood to converse with her. Eventually, the conversation ended, and she flew away. Sinjab and I finished our meal, and we buried a large batch of acorns in various places throughout the woods.

Using my sharp claws, I dug a small hole in the ground. I picked up an acorn, licked it, and placed the treasure into its receptacle. Sinjab saw me struggle slightly, so he came over and helped.

"You wanna make sure the diameter of the hole is at least two inches bigger than the acorn," he explained, his strong paws expanding the hole I had dug. "And once you place the acorn inside, you need to press down on it hard. The earth is soft. Use that to your advantage."

Usually, I detested people giving me unsolicited advice. I had my own way of doing things, the way I wanted. End of story. But with Sinjab...oh, it was a different story altogether! I cherished his every word of advice and every mentoring session he ever gave me. I clung to his words like raindrops cling to the branches of a tree after a storm.

"Like this?" I asked, leaning down on the acorn with my paws.

"More," he said, placing his paws on mine and gently pushing down.

As the earth humbly accepted our acorn, Sinjab patted it down firmly one last time with his nose. We quickly covered it with dirt and leaves. The last thing we needed was unwanted guests feasting on our hard-earned meal.

"You know what fascinates me?" I asked. "The fact that this little acorn can grow into something as great as an oak tree. So much potential in something so small."

"It's a good thing some of our squirrel ancestors forgot where they buried their acorns!" Sinjab laughed. "Otherwise, we may not have found our tree hollow."

"But I don't understand how a squirrel can just forget where they buried their acorn," I mused. "Smell...landmarks...all of that should naturally lead them to it."

"I guess not everyone is at your level," Sinjab teased. "I don't think you've missed a single acorn you've buried."

"Oh, stop it," I said embarrassed, my lips curving into a smile.

"Really, you're a pro. You should start your own class: How to Stash Your Cache, with Mrs. Sasha of

Chirring Woods. Never miss your buried treasure again."

"But I don't want any of those chipmunks in my class," I joked. "I swear, I saw one of them with at least a hundred sunflower seeds in his cheeks!"

"They'll ransack this place before we can say acorn dining."

"We'll keep it undercover, so they don't find out," I laughed. "Sinjab, I'm going to bury this one a little farther up. I'll be back later."

"Why don't I come with you?"

"We'll be more efficient if we split up," I said, taking one of the last acorns in my mouth.

He nodded his head as he continued digging the last few acorns in various spots by the pond.

I ran across the meadow with a large brown acorn in my mouth, letting my keen sense of smell guide me to a pair of yellow aspen trees. I turned around to make sure no one was watching. Digging diligently, I found it: my anniversary gift for Sinjab.

I had used pine needles to string together three acorns by the stem. Using my front teeth, I had artfully gnawed the body of the acorns: two acorns carved to reflect the letter S separated by an acorn carved to reflect a heart. *Sasha Hearts Sinjab.* Nothing could be a better gift or a more powerful symbol of our unshakable love and inseparable bond.

I had spent weeks mastering the curves, having to throw out multiple failed attempts. I would have worked on it for months if I had to. We would hang it in our hollow.

I held it delicately in my mouth and ran towards our acorn tree. Before I climbed up, I chirred softly. Sinjab's chirrs could be heard from a distance. Good – he wasn't home. I climbed up and hid the gift in a corner of our hollow underneath some boxes. In just two days I would present my gift to him. It was going to be the best first-year anniversary any woman could ask for.

# CHAPTER 3: RISKY ROOFTOPS

After a previous hard day of foraging and burying acorns, Sasha and I wanted to unwind and have some fun. We did so through our rooftop adventures. On the outskirts of the woods stood the Straik residence, a large log cabin with a red-tiled roof and brick chimney on the side. We scaled the fence and raced through the back patio, winding in and out of garden chairs, until we reached a pair of pine trees.

We climbed up, the bark soft against our claws. Hopping from branch to branch, we felt the pine needles brush up against our fur. We arrived at one of the top branches which stretched out towards the rooftop.

Powerful strides carried me swiftly across the branch. Just as I felt the branch start to dip, I jumped off and leaped into the air, landing softly on the red tiles. I turned around to see Sasha hesitating. "Don't be afraid. You got this!"

"I'm not sure," she mumbled. "It's a bit of a distance."

"Relax. You've done this before. Just get a head start and let the energy flow through your paws. And right when you feel the branch dip, jump hard and put the pressure on your hind paws."

Sasha nodded as she contemplated her next action. After a few moments, she started to run across the branch and then leap into the air. As she landed on the roof, her claws slid down the tiles towards the gutter. I heard her scream. She was dangling precariously by the gutter, her legs swinging in the air. She was about to fall. I had to act quickly before she slipped.

Without a moment to lose, I hurled myself forward with outstretched arms. I was sliding down the rooftop on my stomach, reaching for her. I grabbed her by both arms and started to lift her up.

"Sinjab!" she screamed.

"I've got you!" I yelled. I slowly pulled her up until she made it safely to the roof's surface. I heard her panting, and I could see her eyes begin to tear.

"That was so scary," she whispered, her nose and whiskers quivering.

I could feel her tremble as I wrapped my arms around her. I comforted her, saying, "I know. But you're safe now."

She whimpered. I held her tight and gently stroked her back.

"You'll be fine," I reassured her.

I'm glad I was there to catch Sasha. She could have really hurt herself without me. At times, she seemed so fragile and sensitive. I felt that it was my duty to protect her no matter what. The desire to be with her, cherish her, and catch her whenever she falls – I suppose that's what it feels like to be in love with another. Those feelings, at that level, I had never felt for any woman in my life, apart from Sasha. Yes, I may have felt some attractions to other women before marriage, but now that I look back, those were just frivolous, superficial feelings. Sasha was my life now. I wanted her to be happy no matter what.

When I felt her breathe normally once more, I released her from my protective embrace. "Do you wanna go home?" I asked gently.

She shook her head.

"Are you sure? We can go back."

"No, I wanna be here with you. I'm fine," she whispered, climbing up the slanted roof. "As long as you're here, I'll be ok."

I would have continued to persuade her to go home, but I knew that once Sasha had made up her mind, there was no changing it.

"Come up here, Sinjab," she called out.

So, I joined her as we zoomed back and forth along the rooftop. We ran circles around each other and jumped up on the chimney. We found such rooftop adventures to be exhilarating. Finding some fallen pine leaves, we tossed them on one another. I almost buried Sasha entirely with leaves before she emerged and chased me to the chimney. We competed with one another to see who could throw pine cones the farthest. I went easy on her and let her win a few times.

After we enjoyed our share of fun, we decided to head back to our acorn tree. I jumped onto the tree branch first. When I was midway, I pushed down on it, lowering the landing for Sasha. After she landed safely, we scurried down the trees.

"Sasha, meet me by the fence," I requested. "I just wanna get some of those berries by the window."

She nodded her head and jumped away towards the fence. As I stood taste-testing some of the berries, I heard the door open. And out stomped an angry, belligerent Mr. Straik, like an ogre emerging from a cave. He staggered around like a crazed lunatic, his head shaking wildly. It was almost going to fall off his neck!

"You little rascal! How many times do I have to tell you filthy pests to stay out of my garden?" he puffed as his chest heaved up and down. His red flannel shirt matched the redness in his face. I could see the veins popping out from his neck. He lunged towards me with his rough, callous hands. I dropped the berries and dashed towards the pine trees, scurrying between his legs. Mr. Straik fell face-first into the garden. As I scampered up the tree, he growled and reached for his broomstick.

"Watch out, Sinjab!" Sasha yelled from afar.

I saw her approaching. "Stay where you are, Sasha!" I ordered. "Don't you dare come over here!"

I felt like a gladiator warrior pitted against a wild beast in an arena. Mr. Straik brandished his weapon, swinging it wildly in the air. I dodged out of harm's way just as the broomstick came crashing down on the trunk of the pine tree. The wild beast continued his savage attack. He held his arms up high, ready to swing again.

"You blasted slimeball!" he fumed. "Stay out of my garden!"

While his weapon was in midair, I ran down the tree into the patio. His broomstick hit the floor as I maneuvered in and out of the garden chairs. He violently kicked the chairs left and right, barricading me in. I was trapped under the table!

I felt my heart racing. If I didn't act quickly, I was done for! I had to fight back – no more defense. Mr. Straik approached with heavy, intimidating steps and overthrew the table, sending it crashing behind me. And just as he was about to snatch me, I leaped onto his shoe and climbed up his trousers. He reached for me through his clothing with his troll-like hands, but I was too quick for such a buffoon. The fool's shirt wasn't tucked in, so I raced up his back and emerged at his collar while he squirmed and fidgeted like a fish out of water.

"Rifling rodents! I'll get you and your little friend," he bellowed, "and skin you two alive!"

I felt a burning rage course through my body. I clenched my teeth and felt my muscles stiffen. My tail twitched uncontrollably. If he wanted to hurt me, fine – but Sasha was absolutely off bounds. I would not tolerate a brutish monster threatening my wife.

I dug my long claws deep into Mr. Straik's neck and then jumped onto his twisted face. Baring my sharp teeth, I sunk them into his cheek, above his rough brown beard. I felt his blood in my mouth. I spat it out in disgust. A guttural roar filled the air.

"Nice hit!" Sasha cheered from the fence. "That'll teach him!"

He grabbed for his face, but I had already jumped down and dashed towards the garden hose sprawled on the edge of the patio. I could hear Sasha encouraging me. "Get him, Sinjab! Show him who's boss!"

As Mr. Straik writhed in pain, I quickly ran circles around him, snaring him with the hose. With his ankles tied up, he sunk to the floor, kneeling down in defeat. The fallen beast growled and snarled. Such would be the end of anyone who dares to threaten Sasha.

"This isn't over yet you rotten rodent! Mark my words, and mark them well, I'm gonna catch you...even if I have to burn the woods and everything in it!"

"Seems like you're a bit tied up at the moment, so I'll leave you alone with your thoughts...and let you unwind a bit."

And with that, I stomped my feet on the patio and ran off to my adoring fan.

"Oh, Sinjab!" she exclaimed. "You were amazing! The way you swerved in and out, dodging all his attacks."

"It wasn't much," I said dismissively, brushing the fur on my shoulder with my paw. "He's just child-play. Barely put up a good fight."

She giggled and nuzzled my neck as she wrapped her tail around me.

"You're so brave. Where did you learn to fight like that?"

"I guess you pick up a thing or two out here in the woods," I responded casually.

"You're my hero, Sinjab," she beamed, looking at me with big, shining eyes. "My hero." Those words could have been carved in acorns for me. I would replay that conversation in my mind over and over again for the whole day. I had made my mark. From that day onward, she would know that I was her protector. A paw to catch her when she falls, a warrior to pounce upon enemies, a force to fend off any danger or threat. I would be there for her, and she would never have to be afraid. I had proven myself a real man to Sasha that day. And that was the victory that really mattered to me.

I accepted what I considered to be a well-deserved kiss. Grabbing her by the forepaw, I gently pulled her along as we raced away from the Straik residence back to our acorn tree.

# CHAPTER 4:
# AN ACORN ANNIVERSARY

Today was the big day. Exactly one year had elapsed since our wedding day, and it had been a beautiful year of marriage. I went down to the pond to bathe and prepare myself for the evening. As I submerged myself in the cool water, I wondered what Sinjab had prepared for me. Some kind of candle-lit dinner by the pond? A festive firefly light show? What kind of roses were waiting for me? Just a few more hours, and I would find out!

As I finished my bath, I combed my fur using a stone comb, applied lipstick using red berries, and sprayed some perfume I had made from pine cone oil. And lastly, I crowned myself with a flower tiara. Looking at my reflection in the pond, I saw a lovely princess staring back at me. Sinjab's princess.

When I returned to our acorn tree later that day, Sinjab was out. I took advantage of the opportunity to make some last-minute touch-ups around the house. Rocking chair in the corner. Bookshelf dusted. And a large bowl of assorted nuts, berries, and acorns. Check, check, and check.

And last, but certainly not least, my anniversary gift for Sinjab. I dug it out of its hiding place and held it proudly in my paws. I heard someone approaching, so I quickly hid the gift behind my back. Sinjab's chirrs drifted up from below. I chirred back.

After a moment, Sinjab appeared at the entrance of the hollow with a bunch of berries in his mouth. He wiped his paws on the doormat and put the berries by the rocking chair.

"Well, if it isn't my lovely Sasha looking all beautiful." He kissed me on the cheek and offered me some berries.

"Before the berries," I said, "I have something for you."

"For me?" he asked surprised. "But it's not my birthday."

I giggled. "Not your birthday gift, silly! Your anniversary gift." I brought forth my acorn-carved gift and presented it to my husband with a big smile. "Happy anniversary, Sinjab!"

He took it in his paws and froze. He wore a blank expression on his face. "Anniversary..." he whispered under his breath, his eyes widening.

Then, there was only silence. We stood like that for about a full minute: Sinjab looking at my gift with bewilderment, and me looking at Sinjab with a hard, cold stare. No gift was reciprocated. No sweet words came my way. Nothing. He glanced up at me, awkwardly scratched the back of his ear, and looked away shyly. Sinjab had forgotten our anniversary.

I tried my best to keep it bottled up inside, but I couldn't help it. Feeling my nose and whiskers quiver, I cried softly.

"Sasha, I'm so sorry."

Before he could continue, I held up a paw to stop him. Shaking my head disapprovingly, I slowly said, "It's not ok. I can't believe you forgot."

"I'll get you something tomorrow, I promise."

I didn't respond.

"Your gift...it's l-lovely...Sasha, th-thank you," he stammered. "S hearts S. That's beautiful. So well thought out and intricate. It's beautiful, just like you."

"Don't try to sweet-talk your way out of this, Sinjab!" I shouted. My sadness quickly became anger. "Maybe if you weren't talking to silly birds all day, you would've remembered!"

"Silly birds?" he asked baffled.

"You heard me. I saw you talking to that Fayra bird. That dumb bird who hops about shamelessly on the branches. My goodness! You think she would have some kind of self-respect."

He opened his mouth to speak, but I wasn't done.

"While I think about our anniversary, you're busy chatting it up with other women!" I yelled, pointing an accusing finger outside our hollow.

"Mrs. Tayra is nothing more than an acquaintance!" Sinjab responded in confusion. "She had nothing to do with me forgetting. I can assure you of that."

"Stop making excuses!" I retorted, wiping away tears.

"I'm sorry, Sasha. I really am. I forgot, and it's all my fault."

"Well, you need to unforget!" I screamed, storming out of the hollow and racing down our oak tree.

Leaping through the meadow, everything became a blur. I dashed in and out of trees, feeling the cold wind lash at my face. A loud cracking noise filled the air every time I landed on a fallen twig. My heart felt heavy, and all I wanted was to be left alone.

Reaching the pond, I flopped down by the rocks and sighed heavily. It was not too long ago that I sat here by the pond, preparing for what I thought would be a romantic, memorable evening. Yet, here I was, disappointed and alone. As I sat there enveloped by the woods, I skipped pebbles across the pond.

I just couldn't understand how Sinjab could forget! It had been on my mind for so long. I had thought long and hard for his gift while it seemed like the thought of gifting me something hadn't even crossed his mind. Almost as if our anniversary wasn't important to him! I felt tears roll down my cheeks as sadness overtook me. I brushed off my tiara with a heavy paw and washed off my lipstick.

And then I thought about that dumb Tayra bird. I tightened my grasp on the final pebble and threw it violently into the water. A loud plunking sound echoed off the trees.

"Stupid bird..." I muttered to myself. "I'll rip off all of your feathers one of these days."

I didn't really think anything was going on between Sinjab and Mrs. Tayra. Even though I knew it was innocent small talk, I couldn't help but feel enraged by it. I wanted Sinjab only to myself.

A disarray of thoughts and emotions ran through me like leaves whirling in a gust of wind. Part of me hated Sinjab at that moment. Because he hurt me. Because I felt my love was unreciprocated. It was almost foolish of me to expect he would remember. I clearly had too high of expectations.

And as more tears rolled down my cheeks, I felt a drizzle of rain from above which eventually became a steady downpour. I shivered, wrapped my arms around myself, and arched my tail overhead to shield myself from the rain.

When I returned to the hollow later that evening, Sinjab was out. Good – I didn't want to see him anyway. I just wanted some space. I picked off a book from the shelf and curled up in the rocking chair. I flipped through the pages of *A Squirrel's Guide to Preparing for Winter* and eventually let sleep take me.

# CHAPTER 5: WOVEN WORKS

When I had returned the previous night to the hollow, I saw Sasha curled up in the rocking chair. Her fur was wet from the rain, or was it from her tears?

I had hung up her gift on the wall overlooking our bed. I wish that I could have reciprocated a gift for her, but it had completely slipped my mind.

With a clouded and preoccupied mind, I jumped from branch to branch in the tangled treetops. My usual swift, balanced movements were now slow, clumsy trudges. Just as I reached one of the oak limbs, I slipped and fell through a web of branches until I landed with a loud thump on a lower bough. I lay there, dazed by the fall. I sighed a deep sigh and closed my eyes.

I thought back to her words. "It's not ok. I can't believe you forgot." And her tears. The whole incident was quite a blow to my ego. And here I was thinking I had proven myself a real squirrel just two days earlier at the Straik residence. She even called me her hero. And then I let her down with such an embarrassing blunder.

"Sinjab, you're a fool," I told myself. "A complete fool."

Regaining my balance, I stood up and looked to the sky to see birds in flight. Did Sasha really think something was going on between me and Mrs. Tayra? Didn't Sasha know by now that my heart belonged only to her?

Feeling angry and disappointed with myself, I lashed out at the bark of the tree with my claws, leaving deep scratch marks. My tail twitched in agitation as I replayed yesterday's incident in my mind. Part of me hated myself. Yesterday should have been an unforgettable anniversary. It would be, but for all the wrong reasons.

I couldn't go back in time, but I would make up for it. I would redeem myself and prove myself a real squirrel no matter what the cost. I paced up and down the branch, thinking long and hard about her gift. I wanted something that would be memorable, something she would cherish. A bouquet of flowers? Too simple, and they would wither over time. A collection of rare stones and gems? Not romantic enough.

Thinking back to her acorn carving, I wanted to gift her something that would complement her own gift. Something that would say *Sinjab Hearts Sasha* back.

"I've got it!" I exclaimed. "A wreath!"

I would craft for her a wreath that would hang around her gift. A wreath that would encircle, surround, and protect her acorn carving.

So, I began my expedition to gather the supplies. Traversing through Chirring Woods, I felt my spirit rise. I was going to bounce back after my pitiful slipup and show Sasha that I could be the romantic husband she wanted me to be.

Weaving in and out of trees, I collected brightly colored leaves of red, orange, and yellow in addition to some small twigs and branches. I set my supplies by the pond and leaped towards the meadow to collect some acorns. I wanted at least five. So, one by one, I took them to the pond, cradling them delicately in my mouth.

I crisscrossed the twigs and branches into a circular base and laced it with the autumn leaves. I then embedded the acorns throughout. It looked good, but it could look better. I glanced towards the pond and saw white water lilies glinting in the sunlight. Diving into the pond, I swam towards them. I felt the cold water permeate my body as my strong kicks propelled me forward. I came upon the prize and gently pushed them towards the bank of the pond using my long tail. I waded ashore and added the lilies to the top of the wreath.

Gazing upon the beauty, I nodded my head approvingly. I hoped Sasha would like it too. It wasn't as intricate as her gift, but I really did give it my all.

I surveyed my surroundings one last time in case anything caught my eye. A bright orange fabric caught in a high branch flapped in the wind.

"I can use it as a bow," I told myself.

I scampered up the trees and leaped through the branches until I reached the fabric. It was a soft plaid fabric that would make a perfect, final addition to my wreath. Returning to the pond, I tied it into a bow and affixed it on the top. And lastly, I touched the wreath to my face and licked the acorns to mark it with my scent.

It was done. I had finished my gift. All that was left was to present it to Sasha. As I prepared to head back to the hollow, I felt my heart skip a few beats and my mouth become dry. I swallowed hard, took a deep breath, and took slow strides towards our oak tree. Once I arrived at the base, I chirred softly. I heard Sasha chirr back. She was home.

I climbed up into our den and saw Sasha rearranging some of the violets hanging from the ceiling.

"Hey there," I greeted her shyly.

"Hey," she said, almost in a whisper.

A full day had passed since my blunder. I hoped that was enough time for her to cool off somewhat.

"I got you something," I announced cheerfully.

I brought forth the wreath from behind my back and presented it to Sasha. What was she going to do with it? I really hoped she wasn't going to throw it out of the hollow. Or worse, at me.

She gazed upon the wreath, and slowly but surely, a big smile spread across her face. Relieved, I exhaled softly.

She took it in her paws. "Sinjab, this is gorgeous."

“It’s the least I could do. I should’ve had it for you yesterday.”

“I like the colors, and the bow too. And it’s not a wreath without acorns,” she said, smelling the wreath and stroking the leaves. “You even put lilies in them.”

“I thought we could —"

“Put it around my gift,” she completed my statement. Walking over to the bed, she hung my wreath around her acorn carving on the wall. “They’re perfect together. They complement one another.”

“Just like us. I’m sorry, Sasha. I’m sorry I forgot about our anniversary.”

“Maybe you did get me something, but you just forgot where you buried it,” she responded in a hushed tone.

“And even when we forget, it can still grow tall and strong,” I said soothingly.

She smiled as I slowly embraced her. "And I'll grow tall and strong with you," she said as she tightened her grasp around me.

I kissed her a tender kiss on her lips. "That you will."

# CHAPTER 6: TROUBLESOME TRIO

I stood by the pond combing my fur. The reflection of the water served as my mirror. I was genuinely pleased with Sinjab's gift yesterday. Granted he should have gotten it for me the day of our anniversary, but it was a well-thought-out gift that meant a lot to me. Good thing for Sinjab I was a flexible woman who was willing to overlook his shortcomings. I made one final touch-up to my fur and put the comb down.

"Tell me again. How did we get stuck babysitting for the day?" Sinjab asked in pain.

"I told you before. Layla and Stefo are visiting family outside the woods, and we as exemplary neighbors, graciously accepted to watch their pups," I responded sharply.

We stood by the pond waiting for our little visitors to arrive.

"I don't recall ever agreeing to this," Sinjab muttered, shaking his head. "I can't imagine a more painful punishment. What did I do to deserve this?"

"Come on, Sinjab. It can't be that bad. It'll be fun!" I said in an attempt to persuade him. "Plus, it's good training for us when we have our own litter —"

"And who said anything about that?" he asked incredulously. "Watching pups is one thing, but having our own is a completely different story!"

"But you must want to have pups of your own one day, don't you?" I inquired with wide eyes.

"Not anytime soon though. I'm comfortable with the way things are now, Sasha. Just me and you. You and me."

But before we could continue our conversation, three young squirrels clad in gray fur arrived with their parents.

"Don't leave me, Mommy!" one of them cried out, clinging onto her mother.

"You'll be fine, Penny," Layla reassured her. "See, look, Payton and Pepper are already having a good time."

Two young squirrels ran circles around Sinjab as he looked around in confusion.

"Thank you again for offering to watch the pups," said Stefo. "It's a bit of a trek to reach the family, and the youngins usually get tired."

"It's our absolute pleasure," I responded cheerfully. "That's what neighbors are for."

"Now I want you three to be on your best behavior for Mrs. Sasha and Uncle Sinjab," said a stern Layla. She had one paw on her waist and another paw pointed at her pups. "If I find out you've been misbehaving…there's to be no nuts for one whole week!"

"One whole week?" the trio chorused.

"You heard me! We'll be back by sunset. You all keep your tails to yourselves. And stay out of trouble."

"Hopefully they won't be too much of a handful," said Stefo hesitantly. He gently pulled on Layla's arm as the two headed off into the woods. I couldn't help but feel like they were relieved to leave.

"It's our absolute pleasure," Sinjab imitated me in a high-pitched voice.

"Stop it!" I chuckled as I threw an acorn at him.

Payton and Pepper got a hold of one another as they tussled on the floor.

"Hey, hey! You two cut it out!" Sinjab ordered, pulling them off one another.

"It's not my fault!" one of them cried out. "Payton is always picking on me."

"I'm not Payton! *You're* Payton!" yelled the other.

"No, I'm Pepper!"

"No, *I'm* Pepper!"

And they went at it again, pulling at each other's fur, each arguing that he was Pepper.

"You can *both* be Pepper," Sinjab declared as he held up each pup in his paws. They clawed in the air as they fidgeted and hissed.

"Mrs. Sasha," Penny said as she tugged on my tail, "why are Payton and Pepper always fighting?"

"I guess that's how they express their love," I reflected. "Seems like bromance has some charm too."

I climbed on top of a small boulder and clapped my paws to get everyone's attention.

"Here's the plan for today," I announced confidently. "We have a couple of different options for you youngins. We can climb trees, play hide and seek, or race across the meadows."

"Climb trees!" yelled Payton.

"Play hide and seek!" boomed Pepper.

"Race across the meadows!" squealed Penny.

Sinjab shook his head as he let the pups free. He frowned and crossed his arms.

"Well then, I suppose we'll just have to do all three. Sinjab and I will lead the way. First is tree-climbing." I took Sinjab by the arm and led him to the trees. "Don't look so thrilled," I said sarcastically, poking him in the ribs. "You were once young and wild like them."

"But I don't think I was that annoying," he muttered.

"Come along, little ones," I called out.

The three squirrels scurried after us as we began our ascent up the tall trees. Jumping up the branches proved to be challenging for Penny as she lagged behind. In one particular crook, she would slide down every time she hopped up. Before I could reach her and offer her a helping paw, Sinjab climbed down and gave her a boost with his head.

"Up you go," he said. "We don't want you falling down, now do we?"

"Again, again!" she giggled, wagging her tail.

"I can't push you up the entire way!"

"You'll learn in time, Penny," I said. "We're tree squirrels after all."

"Uncle Sinjab, how did you learn to be such a great climber?" she asked inquisitively.

"Natural talent," he said.

I saw Payton and Pepper approaching the top of the tree. "Hold on you two. Wait for us." We scampered up, Sinjab giving Penny an occasional boost. When we reached the top, it was time to jump to the other tree.

"Now is the exciting part," I stated. "We've jumped up the branches. But now it's time to jump from tree to tree."

Payton and Pepper clapped and whistled in excitement.

"I bet I can jump farther than you, Payton," boasted Pepper.

"In your dreams. I'm gonna set the world record right here for longest leap," declared Payton.

"I believe I've already set that world record," Sinjab stated.

"Mrs. Sasha, I'm scared," Penny whimpered as she tugged on my tail.

"No need to be scared, dear. You can hop on my back for the jump." I lowered my tail for her. She climbed up and wrapped her arms around my neck, holding me tight.

"I'll go first!" Payton announced as he bounded across the bough and leaped into the air. He landed safely on the branch of the next tree as he hooted in joy. "Beat that!"

"I'll show you!" said a determined Pepper. "World champ coming through – make way!"

And Pepper darted across the branch, flung himself into the air, and tumbled onto one of the lower branches. Payton bellowed in laughter, almost falling off the branch.

"What was *that*?" Payton jeered. "You barely missed the floor on that one."

"Payton, be nice," I said sternly. "You did great Pepper – keep it up!"

"The wind blew me down," Pepper muttered as he paced awkwardly on the branch. Sinjab gestured for me to jump. "Ladies first. Remember, use your tail for balance. You got this."

I got a running start, and right when I felt the branch start to dip, I leaped into the air with outstretched paws. I felt Penny's grasp tighten around my neck as the tree drew near. I breathed deeply, straightened my tail, and landed gracefully on one of the branches.

"Wow, that was amazing Mrs. Sasha!" Penny squealed in delight. "You were like a ballerina!"

I lowered my tail and let her climb down. Next was Sinjab's turn. And with effortless strides, he dashed across the branch, glided in the air, and landed on a high branch.

"How did you do that?" Payton asked in astonishment, his jaw dropping.

"He must be a flying squirrel!" Pepper chimed in. "It's like he had wings."

"What'd I say? Natural talent," Sinjab responded.

We zipped down the trees and found ourselves in the meadows once more. I imagined such a day to be our routine life if Sinjab and I had a litter of our own. I could understand some of Sinjab's concerns as young pups carried a heavy responsibility, but it also added color to one's life. When Sinjab and I became older, I wanted someone there to take care of us.

"It's my turn to pick the game now," Penny stated, "and I wanna play hide and seek."

"Payton is so bad at this game that he couldn't even find himself," taunted Pepper.

"Why don't you go fall off another tree," retorted Payton smugly.

Before the boys could tackle one another, Sinjab held each one by the fur of his neck. "A nice thing about this game is that everyone hides in *separate* places. That means that you two will be *far* away from each other. Now I'll be the seeker and you all hide. You guys have twenty seconds."

As Sinjab covered his eyes, we all scattered about in the meadows. I urged Penny to hide with me in the bushes by the pond, but she insisted on hiding behind a tree instead.

"Ok, but don't go too far," I whispered. "Stay where I can see you."

Penny nodded her head and ran towards a nearby tree. Payton buried himself under a sea of acorns while Pepper perched on a tree branch behind some leaves.

"Seventeen, eighteen, nineteen, nineteen and a half, twenty!" Sinjab announced. "Tree squirrel or not, here I come!"

I peeked through the bushes to see Sinjab prowling through the meadows, his tail high in the air. "You can only hide for so long my young ones...before you are discovered...and brought back to me..." came his spooky voice. "Fallen acorns all around us. But a bulging pile is suspicious indeed..."

We could hear giggles and see the pile of acorns shake.

"And thus, a tree squirrel emerges from the acorn hill!" Sinjab yelled as he grabbed a laughing Payton out from underneath the acorns.

"How did you find me?" Payton moaned.

"I could hear you from miles away. But the question now becomes, where dost thy brother, little Pepper, hideth himself? Dost he look down upon us from yonder?"

Sinjab pointed a finger straight at Pepper who hid high in the branches.

"Oh man! I thought I had cauliflowered myself good," grumbled a despondent Pepper as he shuffled down the tree.

I turned around to check on Penny behind the tree. The little one had vanished! I looked to the other trees, but there was no sign of her at all.

I dashed out from behind the bush and called out, "Penny! Where are you?"

"I believe that's my job," Sinjab said from across the pond. "Maybe we need to have a refresher on how hide and seek works."

"I'm looking for Penny," I explained.

"Yeah...so am I. We're at the 'seeking' part now unless I'm mistaken."

"No, I mean Penny is gone. I told her to stay there by the tree. She's run off, and I don't know where she is!"

"Relax, we'll find her. How far can she possibly have gone? Let's split up. You take Payton, and I'll take Pepper."

So, we split up in search of Penny. I felt my heart race and my mouth become dry. I would never forgive myself if anything happened to her. And I didn't think her parents would ever forgive me either. How could I expect to be a mother when I couldn't even keep an eye out on a young pup for a few measly minutes?

"Penny! Penny!" I hollered, weaving in and out of the trees.

"Mrs. Sasha, is Penny gone?" asked Payton as he followed along.

"No, dear. She's fine, she's just....exploring the woods, I suppose." I tried to reassure him just as much as myself.

"If we can't find Penny, will it just be me and Pepper?"

"Stop that. We *will* find her. And you'll stay as the troublesome trio that you are." I began to understand the stern tone Layla used when she was giving instructions to her pups. I also began to understand the hesitancy in Stefo's voice as he hoped the pups wouldn't be too much of a handful.

How could I have been so careless? I should have kept Penny with me by the bushes. Parenting was obviously much harder than it seemed. It wasn't too long ago that I thought I had done an admirable job delivering her across the trees. And now I didn't even know where she was!

I paused and held my nose up high in the air. "Wait, I think I smell her scent." I felt a glimmer of hope. "Come along, Payton."

"I hope that we find her. I don't want Pepper finding our sister. He doesn't deserve it," Payton murmured.

We searched high and low through the trees, her name echoing in the woods. As we scouted the area, we followed her scent with high hopes. Darting across the soft earth, we heard a faint weeping sound.

"Penny!" I exclaimed, dashing forward. The noise grew louder...and stronger. "I'm coming, Penny!"

We eventually stumbled upon a distraught Penny hanging upside down from a tree, her tail wrapped around a low-hanging branch.

"What in the world are you doing up there?" I asked, trying my best not to snap at her. "Why did you run off like that? You gave us all quite a scare."

"Because we were playing hide and seek," she cried out. "My tail was hiding, and I couldn't find it. So, I went out in search for it."

My eyes narrowed, and I stood with both paws on my hips. "Now you come down right now, little missy. No excuses. Right now, I said!"

Penny scrambled down as Payton nudged her with his nose.

"Don't you ever do that again, you hear me? It's not cute, and it's not funny. You could have been hurt or eaten. There are snakes in these woods!"

She looked down bashfully and nodded her head. I took her into my arms, and we returned to the pond. Upon arriving, I chirred to beckon Sinjab. He chirred back, and soon, I saw him emerge from the trees with Pepper.

As I released Penny from my arms, Pepper raced forward and gave his sister a hug. She giggled, and the trio tumbled and twisted over one another.

"Young Penny was wandering off in the woods," I said, my eyes tearing.

"I'm sorry, Mrs. Sasha. I'm sorry, Uncle Sinjab," Penny apologized.

"It's a good thing someone didn't mistake you as an acorn and bury you," Sinjab stated. "We may not have seen you until the winter. Now how about you three go race in the meadows – where we can see you. While me and Mrs. Sasha have some peace and quiet. Off you go. All three of you. And play nice."

The three pups raced in the meadows as their laughter bounced off the trees. Sinjab came and placed a comforting arm around me as he wiped my tears away with his paw.

"Sasha, it's ok. What's done is done. The important thing is that she's safe."

"But it shouldn't have happened. I should've kept a closer eye on her."

“You tried your best. That’s just how pups are. Don’t beat yourself up.”

“What kind of mother will I be, Sinjab, when I can’t even keep an eye out on one pup?”

“An amazing mother. And I don’t doubt that. Not in the least bit.”

Sinjab led me towards a large boulder by the pond and pulled me under his arm. We saw the three pups race up and down the meadows, pulling each other’s tails, and barking at one another.

“Imagine having a bunch of mini Sinjabs and mini Sashas running around Chirring Woods,” I mused.

Sinjab looked away.

“Sinjab, won’t you have a litter, for my sake?” I pleaded.

No response.

"Don't you want someone to take care of us in our old age?"

After a long moment of silence, he responded. "I'm comfortable with our way of life now. I don't want it to change. At least not now."

"But down the line?"

He looked me deep in the eyes with a stoic stare.

"If it means that much to you...then...then..."

"Then?" I asked, staring at him with big imploring eyes.

"Then...I'll maybe...possibly think about it," he said, his lips curving up ever so slightly.

"Sinjab!"

He laughed and wrapped his tail around mine.

"There's no rush, Sasha. When the time is right, we'll have our own litter."

And with that, he kissed me a tender kiss. As the day passed on and we reached early evening, Layla and Stefo returned from their journey. The little ones had twigs in their paws, and they were sword fighting.

"Mommy! Daddy!" they all yelled, running towards their parents.

"Thank you so much to the both of you for watching them," Layla said as she stroked their fur. "How did everything go?"

"Let's just say they kept us busy," I said, wishing to avoid the topic of a lost Penny altogether.

"Pa, you should've seen the jump I made today. I think it was the longest distance I've ever jumped," said an excited Pepper.

"Pa, I jumped farther. Even Uncle Sinjab said so himself," boasted Payton. "He said I was the best tree squirrel he's ever seen."

"He did not! You liar," countered Pepper.

"I'm sure you both did great," chuckled Stefo. "It's a good thing you youngins had such great teachers today."

"Mommy, can we play with Mrs. Sasha and Uncle Sinjab again?" asked Penny.

"If you and your brothers didn't cause them too much trouble, then maybe they'll consider it," Layla responded.

We said our goodbyes, and they raced off into the trees. As Sinjab and I returned to our hollow, we collapsed on our bed, exhausted from a long day.

"Boy, oh boy. Pups just drain your energy," Sinjab said. "I'm wiped out."

"Tell me about it. Pups are fun, but they can give you a headache." I closed my eyes and rested a paw over my forehead. "Sinjab, would you get me some berries please? They always help whenever I have a headache."

Sinjab looked in the basket for some berries, but we had run out.

"Let me go look by the pond," he offered. After a few minutes, he returned empty-handed.

"They've been picked clean. Must be those pesky chipmunks," he said. "Let me go over to the Straik residence and get some."

"No, stay here with me. It's getting late anyway. I can wait until tomorrow."

"Are you sure? I don't mind going now."

I nodded my head and beckoned him to come lay with me. As the starry night blanketed Chirring Woods, we fell asleep in each other's arms and drifted into a much-needed slumber.

# CHAPTER 7:

# CRACKS AND CREAKS

I had to get the berries for Sasha no matter what. I didn't want her to be in any pain. She said her head still hurt this morning. Her pain was my pain. Dashing through the meadows, I reached the Straik residence and scaled the fence. I leaped towards the garden of berries only to find a disheartening sight: all the berries had vanished!

It was just a few days ago that I saw the garden teeming with berries. How could they just disappear like that? Where could they have gone? I smelled the scent of the berries close by, emanating from above – I was sure of it.

I turned around to climb up the pine trees only to see myself staring right back at me. It was my reflection from an odd, shiny metal that was pinned to the base of the trees. It looked like some kind of peculiar device to keep away UFOs. After sliding down the slippery material several times, I deduced it was meant to keep me away. I tried to gnaw at it, but the metal was too strong. I tried to pull away the nails, but they were too deeply embedded in the bark.

I needed to reach the rooftop so I could better home in on the scent of berries. But how?

"Think, Sinjab, think," I told myself. "For Sasha."

I looked around for the broomstick Mr. Straik had attacked me with, but it was nowhere in sight. Otherwise, I would have used it as a ladder to reach the higher branches. I saw the garden chairs neatly surrounding the table on the patio.

"I think I have an idea."

I pushed one of the garden chairs closer to the trees. It wasn't tall enough for me to reach the branches, but I could use it as a pivot point. Scrambling onto the table, I darted quickly across and leaped towards the top of the chair. Right when I started to feel the chair lean back, I let the momentum propel me forward as I threw myself towards a low-hanging branch. The chair clattered to the ground just as I landed safely on the limb.

I hurried up the tree and jumped towards the roof. Pacing back and forth along the red tiles, I sensed the presence of the berries. I followed my nose until I reached the edge of the roof which had a small crevice between the tiles and the wall. I peered in with inquisitive eyes only to see darkness. My nose and whiskers twitched as I inhaled the potent aroma of fresh berries. They were here, right underneath the rooftop.

I squeezed myself through the small crack to come upon a dark, dusty room. Stale, stuffy air filled my nose. There was just enough sunlight seeping through the crevice to dimly light the mysterious room under the roof.

"What is this place?" I asked myself, brushing off spider webs from my fur. "I've never been here before."

The wood floor creaked underneath my paws as I meandered through a maze of large cardboard boxes and piles of clothing. Stacks of books and magazines lay scattered about. I stumbled across what seemed to be a photo album of Mr. Straik. I flipped through to see a burly man in a red lumberjack shirt holding up an axe. He stood next to a fallen tree with a wide, scornful smile plastered across his face. I looked up to see the same axe hanging on the wall.

I felt a chill go down my spine. All I wanted to do was find the berries, leave this spooky place, and return to Sasha. I used my sense of smell to guide me through the new territory. The berries were near. I roamed in and out of the aisles...left...right...over this stack of books...through that pile of clothing. Until I found them.

Fresh, juicy berries staring me right in the eye. Dead ahead. I felt my spirit rise as my eyes widened and my tail swung back and forth in excitement. The red berries were like shining rubies calling out to me. I stared at them with covetous eyes.

Proceeding cautiously, I lay one paw in front of the other. I felt my whiskers twitch. Almost there. And just as I grasped the prize, I heard a loud clanking noise pierce the air. I whirled around to see a kind of gate barring my way!

"No...," I whispered.

I sprinted in the direction I had come from and threw myself against the gate, but it wouldn't budge. I ran to the left and right, but walls blocked my escape. I ran to the back, but it was a dead end. I tried to jump up, but a metal ceiling threw me back down. I was trapped!

And then I heard the sound of laughter. A soft chuckle. Then, a roaring laughter that ricocheted off the walls. It was like the enemy had multiplied and was attacking me from all directions.

"Well, what do we have here? An uninvited guest."

A figure emerged from the darkness like a stealthy shadow coming out of hiding. Mr. Straik approached with slow, deliberate footsteps until he loomed overhead.

"Didn't anyone ever teach you not to go snooping in other people's attics?"

He held a flashlight in his hand which he pointed at me. I held my paws up to block the piercing light.

"Tsk, tsk. Rodents must not trespass. Trespassers will be persecuted!"

He shined the light on his face which revealed a vengeful sneer and a crazed look in his eyes. His crackling laughter filled the air as his body flailed around violently. I could see saliva drooling from his mouth, foaming at the edges. And on his cheek, I saw a large gash.

I raced back and forth, trying to free myself. I hurled myself against the walls but to no avail. I gnawed at the metal rods, but they were too thick. Scratching the roof with my claws did nothing for my escape either. My body wouldn't stop shaking. My tail wouldn't stop twitching. I felt my heart thrashing in my chest. I could almost feel it in my throat.

"Try all that you can you blasted slimeball, but you'll never escape," Mr. Straik snickered. "Pity you didn't bring that little friend of yours." He bent down so he was eye level with me. "But there's always next time!"

"Let me out right now you ugly oaf!" I hissed as I thrashed about, clawing at the walls. "Don't you even think of laying a finger on her!"

"Rifling rodents to be gone forever!" he snorted, wiping away foam from his mouth.

"Just wait until I get my claws on you!" I yelled. "You'll be dinner for the dogs!"

Darkness then engulfed me as Mr. Straik shrouded my prison with a large piece of cloth. Was this how my life would end? Who would take care of Sasha?

I felt myself being raised. There were heavy footsteps. I then heard the opening of a door and Mr.

Straik grunting. A sharp jerking movement shook me up and down, making me lose my balance. Where was the wild beast taking me?

I heard another door creak open, and then I felt the biting wind of the cold autumn air. Was he going to get his axe? Would I be his next meal?

"Say goodbye to your pathetic life, you little runt," Mr. Straik chuckled. "And who knows, maybe your little friend will be joining you soon."

"You touch Sasha, and it will be the last thing you'll ever do!" I roared.

I toppled upside down as I heard a loud crashing noise of metal on metal. I scrambled to regain my balance as the wind blew by and partially removed the cover. I looked around desperately only to see tools and poles. An engine came to life with a rumbling groan. I was in the back of Mr. Straik's pickup truck!

The car chugged along, bouncing up and down a bumpy road. As the car sped away, I peered through my small window to see Chirring Woods become nothing more than a small speck in the distance. My heart sank as the nightmare carried on. Where was he taking me? What was he going to do with me? Would I ever see my beloved again?

After some time, we came to a halt as the engine turned off. I heard the crunching footsteps of Mr. Straik as he approached the back of his truck. He removed the cover on my prison and hauled me up. I saw other cars lined up and humans walking about. Glancing around, I saw a sign that read "Ashjar Forest."

Mr. Straik walked towards some trees and placed my prison on the grass. He slowly raised the gate and kicked the metal structure.

"Scram, you filthy scumbag! Get outta here!" he yelled. "And don't let me see your scrawny little face again."

I bolted out like lightning, running like I had never run before. My surroundings became nothing more than a blur as I sprinted through unknown territory. I turned around, expecting Mr. Straik to be chasing me. But interestingly enough, I saw him climb back into his car and drive off.

I spotted some trees up ahead, so I scurried up as fast as I could. I jumped from branch to branch until I reached the top. My shaking paws held the limb so tight it was almost going to snap under the pressure. I could barely maintain my balance with such a fidgeting tail.

Despite my own frenzied predicament, my thoughts returned only to Sasha. I was stripped from the love of my life. I longed to be with her, to have her in my arms. Was she safe? Was Mr. Straik going to come after her?

I had to return to Chirring Woods no matter what. I would retrace my footsteps and be with Sasha once more. It would be difficult because my vision was mostly obscured during the drive, but I would find a way.

As my worries and fear took hold, I heard a gruff voice from below. "Oi, you up there!"

I looked down to see a raccoon staring at me with angry eyes. The black fur around his eyes made him look like a bandit. He brushed his long white whiskers with his pointed claws as he observed me from afar.

"I ain't seen you here before. Yer comin with me, mister."

Before I could respond, he took out a slingshot and pelted me with a rock. As it hit my head, I felt myself lose consciousness and fall off the branch.

# CHAPTER 8: EMPTY ECHOES

The entire night had passed, and Sinjab still hadn't returned to the hollow. Where in the world could he be? Did something happen? There was never a night in which he did not return. I had a very bad feeling about it.

My headache had subsided a bit, so I decided to climb down the oak tree and search for Sinjab. I climbed up the trees, passed by the pond, and searched through the meadows. I smelled his scent, but no sign of Sinjab anywhere.

He said that he was heading to the Straik residence to find the berries, so I decided to look there. I leaped through the woods until I reached the outskirts and came upon the Straik residence. Scaling the fence, I headed over to the patio area by the pine trees. Sinjab's scent grew stronger. He was here recently.

Looking over to the pair of pine trees, I saw strange sheets of metal pinned to the bark. They glinted in the bright sunlight as I cautiously circled the trees. I tried climbing up, but I kept slipping down. Spotting a broomstick, I brought it over and leaned it up against the trees. I scampered up the broomstick until my claws reached the bare bark.

I smelled a fresh scent as I paced up and down the branches. I would say that Sinjab was here in these trees just yesterday. I chirred softly, hoping to hear him chirr back. But there was no response. I chirred again, this time exhaling more forcefully. Silence ensued. I continued chirring until my low trilling voice filled the entire premise with whistles, chirps, and kuks.

"Sinjab, where are you!?" I called out desperately, feeling out of breath and distressed.

I rubbed my face against the branches to mark it with my own scent. If Sinjab were to come back to the trees, at least he would know I was here looking for him.

"Excuse ma'am, are you looking for someone?" a high-pitched voice asked from below.

I looked down to see a small chipmunk taking cover under one of the garden chairs. Streaks of black and white fur ran down her brown back, her tail wagging behind her.

"I'm looking for my husband. He was here yesterday," I responded.

"Yesterday…where was I yesterday? Wait a minute, I was here!"

"Did you see a squirrel here?" I asked, feeling a glimmer of hope creep inside. "With brownish-gray fur like mine. Bushy tail and round ears."

"Let me think. As a matter of fact, now that you mention it, I did! A big squirrel climbing through those same trees you're in right now."

"You did!? Oh, that's such a relief!" I exclaimed.

"I saw him climb up the trees to the rooftop. I was minding my own business down here, scavenging for sunflower seeds."

"And after the rooftop, where did you see him?" I pleaded.

"Well, I went out to the front to see what I could find over there," she continued. "And after some time, I saw Mr. Straik marching out of the front door with some kind of cloaked box in his hand. I couldn't see what was inside, but it kept shaking. Almost like someone was trying to get out."

The chipmunk came out from underneath the garden chair and came closer to the trees.

"I don't know what was underneath the cloak," she explained, "but I heard a voice. It said something like, touch Sasha...last thing you'll ever do...and then Mr. Straik put it in his car and drove off."

I felt my heart sink and a cold chill run through my body. My breathing stopped and my tail froze. It was almost like someone had thrown a bucket of ice on me. Sinjab was captured!

"Miss, are you alright up there?" the chipmunk asked.

I dashed down the broomstick and leaped across the grass to the front of the house.

"Sinjab! Sinjab!" I yelled.

I saw Mr. Straik's truck parked in the driveway. I clambered up and chirred desperately. Rummaging through the tools and buckets, I searched for some kind of message Sinjab may have left me. There was nothing, only his scent. What did Mr. Straik do with him? Was Sinjab still...? I stopped myself from such morbid thoughts as I wiped back flowing tears. I climbed out of the truck to find the chipmunk again.

"It makes me awfully sad to see you crying like such, Miss," she said, patting me on the shoulder.

"My husband, he's gone!" I cried out.

"Maybe we can find him. It seems like Mr. Straik was taking him somewhere else," she responded.

"But where to?"

"Ahh...that's the question, isn't it?"

Feeling distraught, I decided to head back to the hollow to collect my thoughts.

"Thank you for your help," I said with a heavy sigh as I turned towards the woods. "What was your name again?"

"Whisty."

"Well, thank you, Whisty."

Back in our hollow, I collapsed onto the rocking chair, feeling drained of all energy. It was almost like I was trapped in a ghastly nightmare. I couldn't believe Sinjab was gone. And what was even more distressing was the fact that I didn't even know where he was or if he was ok.

I shuddered at the thought and told myself that Sinjab was fine. The chipmunk had explained that Mr. Straik had put Sinjab in his car, which probably meant he was just taking him somewhere else.

What was I to do? Was I to set out in search of him, or was I to stay here in Chirring Woods waiting for him to return? What if I were to leave when he comes back? He would find me gone. I decided to stay in the woods, hoping he would return soon.

The days became weeks as I waited patiently in Chirring Woods. Searching the woods became my daily routine as I climbed the trees, paced up and down the meadows, and visited the pond. I returned to the Straik residence a few times as well only to return empty-handed. And all the while, my humming chirrs rolled through the woods like leaves caught in a breeze. My empty echoes must have filled every crevice in the woods by now. Chirring Woods felt cold without Sinjab. It just wasn't the same.

Layla tried her best to comfort me. "Maybe he just got lost. He's probably looking for you right now. Give him more time."

"I'm not sure. It's been so long. Two full weeks. Feels like forever," I said.

We were climbing a tree together with Penny. She had grown much bigger and was able to climb up the branches almost effortlessly. "Mrs. Sasha, I'm sorry to hear about Uncle Sinjab. We all miss him so much."

"Yeah, so do I. The thought of losing him like this never crossed my mind."

"Stefo has been keeping an eye out for him as well," Layla stated as we reached the treetop. "If he finds any trace of him, we'll make sure to let you know right away."

I nodded my head. Looking out over the woods, I remembered the times that Sinjab would take me up to the treetops. They were such beautiful moments. If only he were here now.

"Why don't we form an expedition?" suggested Penny. "We all set out in search of Uncle Sinjab. We leave Chirring Woods and explore the unknown. He'll be so happy when he sees us!"

The thought of leaving home had crossed my mind several times. "But you can't leave Chirring Woods, silly. It's a jungle out there. Besides, my husband wouldn't want you leaving the woods."

"Stefo and I really would set out, Sasha, but I'm afraid with three pups, we just wouldn't be able to," Layla explained. "Please forgive us for not being able to help more."

"It's fine. Sinjab would want you all here anyway, safe and sound." We were making our way down the tree towards the meadow. "But I do think about leaving at times. To find him."

"If you're leaving, then I wanna come with you, Mrs. Sasha!" insisted Penny who was leading the way.

"Not in your wildest dreams!" I said, shutting down the idea. "A young squirrel like yourself can't go out into the wild like that. It's too dangerous."

"But I wanna help find Uncle Sinjab. We need to bring him home," she protested.

"A noble intention, Penny, but Mrs. Sasha is right," stated Layla. "The wild is no place for a wee pup like yourself."

"I'm not a pup anymore! I'm a grown squirrel now," she muttered. "But Mrs. Sasha, are you really going to leave Chirring Woods all by yourself?"

We had reached the meadows, and it was getting late. I really didn't know what I should do, whether I should stay or leave. I turned to Penny and said, "If I were to leave Chirring Woods...it would be the bravest thing I've ever done in my life."

"You'll say goodbye first, right? You wouldn't just leave without telling us, would you?" Penny asked, her eyes filling with tears.

"Of course, dear. I would say my goodbyes first," I said, imagining the waterworks of such an occasion.

"If there's anything we can do to help at all, Sasha, do let us know. I really wish we could be of more help," Layla said apologetically.

"Thank you, Layla, I appreciate it."

As Penny and her mother returned to their hollow, I returned to mine.

As I tarried in the woods for the third week, I realized that many of the trees had shed their leaves, almost like they felt too drained and weak to hold onto them anymore. Like they had lost interest in something they once deemed so wondrous and magical. What was once a vibrant mosaic of autumn colors was now a drab and barren canvas.

Howling wind rattled the bare trees which cloaked the meadows with skeleton-like shadows. The dark figures veered left and right with menacing hands as they tried to seize me. I shrunk away, wishing with all my heart that Sinjab were here to comfort me and protect me. I missed everything about him, from his warmth and scent to his charm and humor. But what I missed the most about him was his voice. His soothing voice and melodious chirrs that once put my sadness and worries at bay. I would give anything to hear it once more.

The longer I stayed in Chirring Woods, the more I came to an unequivocal realization: my enduring attachment to the woods was merely an extension of my enduring attachment to Sinjab. And with Sinjab gone, the woods had lost its charm and appeal altogether. I didn't feel the rush of energy I always felt. I was no longer enthralled by the trees, the meadows, or the pond. Instead, I felt my energy draining as I became weaker by the day. The woods only amplified the gaping emptiness I felt within.

Chirring Woods would never be the same without him, and nor would I. And just as the leaves drifted away from the trees they once held so dear, I too needed to drift away.

I decided to leave Chirring Woods. Whether Sinjab was out there or not, I couldn't stay here. It just wasn't good for me anymore. I would depart and search for Sinjab. Preparing my knapsack, I gathered some nuts and acorns along with a container of water. As I wiped back a torrent of tears, I prepared to say goodbye to the hollow. I looked upon our gifts hanging on the wall, wishing I could take them with me, but I knew it would just slow me down. Plucking off an acorn from Sinjab's wreath, I laced it with a pine needle and wore it around my neck. I took one last look at our den, turned around, and scampered down the oak tree.

I had told Layla and Stefo that I would be leaving earlier that week. They said they would meet me by the pond to say their farewells.

"Do you really have to leave, Mrs. Sasha?" whimpered Payton.

"We want you to stay here with us. Who will look after us when Mommy and Daddy are gone?" sniveled Pepper, his ears drooping.

"I leave because I must. I need to find Uncle Sinjab," I explained gently, my paw reaching up to my acorn necklace.

Penny ran towards me and threw herself into my arms. "We'll miss you so much, Mrs. Sasha. I wish you didn't have to leave." I felt her tears on my fur. "I do hope you'll come back soon."

Payton and Pepper joined in for a group hug. Three wailing pups embraced me with strong arms. I tried my best not to break down in tears myself. I wanted to be strong for their sake.

"We wish you the best, Sasha," Stefo said somberly. "Hope you can find Sinjab and be happy again."

"Sasha, my dear, take care. We'll be here in the woods if you need anything at all," Layla said lovingly as she gently pulled her pups away. "Now my darlings, Mrs. Sasha needs to leave."

"You three be good for Mommy and Daddy, you hear me? No wandering about alone," I instructed the friendly trio.

The pups and their parents said their goodbyes as they stood waving by the pond. I waved one last time and disappeared into the trees.

As I approached the outskirts of Chirring Woods, I took one last look at what was once our sanctuary. Tears rolled down my face as my nose and whiskers quivered. A cold gust of wind suddenly ripped through the woods as the trees moaned and the dead leaves dispersed. I put one paw in front of the other and began my journey into the unknown. In search of the one whom I always loved. In search of my other half. To be whole once more.

www.ingramcontent.com/pod-product-compliance
Lightning Source LLC
LaVergne TN
LVHW051014080826
845145LV00009B/2625